To my dad, Nick Cross, for bringing me under the pier when I was little,
and to Ruby, Sophie, and Jon for helping me remember how magical it still is.

—N.C.B.

For Jacob, Mica, Calder, and Mom. Thank you.

—R.S.

The author donates a portion of her proceeds to HEAL THE BAY AQUARIUM,
an educational nonprofit located under the Santa Monica Pier that gives visitors
the chance to see 100 local species and touch as many as they dare.
Visit www.healthebay.org to learn about the many ways HEAL THE BAY
works to protect the sea life of the Santa Monica Bay.

Text copyright © 2020 by Nell Cross Beckerman
Illustrations copyright © 2020 by Rachell Sumpter
Book design by Melissa Nelson Greenberg

Library of Congress Cataloging-in-Publication Data available.
ISBN: 978-1-944903-86-2

Printed in China.

10 9 8 7 6 5 4 3 2 1

Cameron Kids is an imprint of Cameron + Company

Cameron + Company
Petaluma, California
www.cameronbooks.com

DOWN UNDER THE
PIER

BY NELL CROSS BECKERMAN

ILLUSTRATED BY RACHELL SUMPTER

cameron kids

Up on the pier,
we ride the giant Ferris wheel,
we scream on the roller coaster,
we gobble clouds of cotton candy.

Wood planks creak as we walk in the sun.

Up on the pier,
we pass carousel horses,
and we dash for the
chance to ride the lone goat.

Up and down and round and round.

PRIZES

Up on the pier,
we feed the machines,
roll Skee-Balls, whack moles,
and trade our tickets for toys.

Lights flash, bells ding, buzzers zing.

Our pockets empty, quarters spent.
Is the fun all done? Maybe . . . for some.

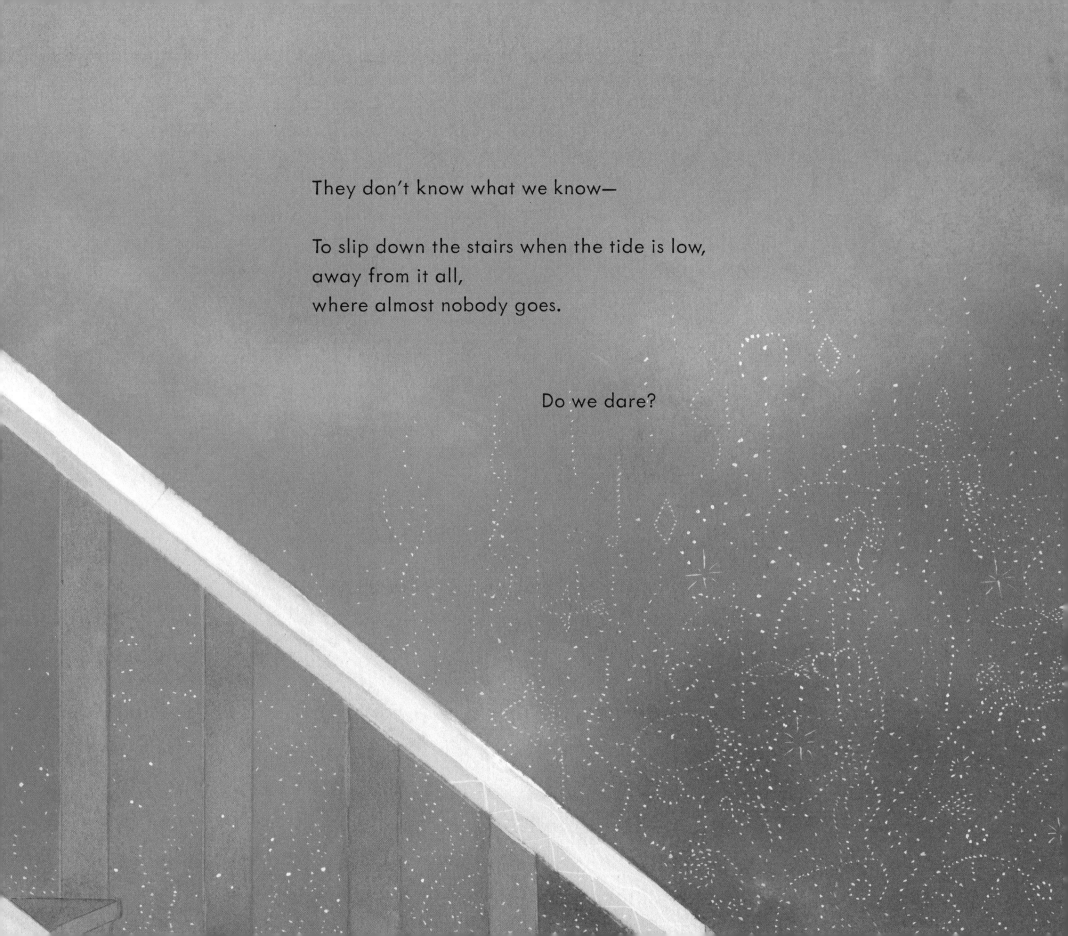

They don't know what we know—

To slip down the stairs when the tide is low,
away from it all,
where almost nobody goes.

Do we dare?

Down under the pier,
it's dark and cool.
We inhale sea spray
and squish slimy sand through toes.

Goose bumps on sun-kissed skin.

Down under the pier,
we chase grey waves
and hear the crashing curls thunder.
We pause and listen, then . . .

yelling, howling, we race through the echoes.

Down under the pier,
when the tide hides
we find creatures clinging.

Mussels, barnacles, sea stars,
and anemones festoon a forest of pilings.

We look
and wonder . . .
Is it alive?
Will it bite?
Will it pinch?
Will it pierce?
Will it do anything at
all if we just gently
poke it?

Down under the pier,
receding waves reveal
bubbles on the sand.
Before the waves return, we dig.

Handfuls of crabs tickle and terrify.

Sanderlings scamper,
their stick legs a blur.
Can we catch them?

Almost! Almost! Always just out of reach.

Down under the pier,
we hunt for ropes of kelp,
play a slippery game of tug-of-war,
and stomp on the poppers.

We are seaweed monsters.

Down under the pier,
we hide and seek
and collect seashell souvenirs.

Our pockets full, rich with treasures.

Down under the pier,
in the glow of the low sun,
there are no lines, no seat belts,
no closing times.

Fun is free,
and the world is ours.

WHAT CAN YOU FIND DOWN UNDER THE PIER?

The tall pilings under the pier are home to animals who live in the intertidal zone. These special creatures live part of their lives underwater, during high tide, and part of their lives out of water, during low tide. Clustered together, they help each other survive in an intertidal community.

Check for low tide and maybe you'll spy . . .

ACORN BARNACLES close their shells tightly, trapping water inside, preventing them from drying up. They breathe oxygen and eat plankton from this stored water, while their tough shells protect them from hungry birds.

ANEMONES have no shell, so they squeeze between other animals for protection. Long tentacles around their mouths catch crabs, snails, and small fish. Gently poke and watch them squeeze!

GOOSENECK BARNACLES sometimes move if you touch them. Are you brave enough to try? These pointy crustaceans are related to crabs and lobsters.

MOLE CRABS live in the swash zone of the sand. To feed, these sand crabs dig backward, down and down. As the waves flow over them, their antennae uncoil, trapping yummy plankton. Look for the bubbles on the sand and dig quickly!

MUSSELS stick to pilings with thick, sticky threads. They close up tight like barnacles and also eat plankton. These mollusks are clams' cousins.

SEA STARS devour an average of eighty mussels annually and can live for twenty years. So how many mussels does one sea star eat in a lifetime?

SNAILS hang on with one big foot and use their hard shells for protection from waves and predators.